THE Angel WITHIN

K. C. Copperfield

BALBOA
PRESS

A DIVISION OF HAY HOUSE

Balboa Press books may be ordered through booksellers or by contacting:

Balboa Press
A Division of Hay House
1663 Liberty Drive
Bloomington, IN 47403
www.balboapress.com
1 (877) 407-4847

Print information available on the last page.

ISBN: 978-1-9822-1077-9 (sc)
ISBN: 978-1-9822-1078-6 (e)

Balboa Press rev. date: 09/04/2018

This book is dedicated to
all the beautiful Angels in my
life, past, present and to come.
Thank you for all the love
and inspiration.

Contents

CHAPTER 1

Things That Go Bump

L ate on a warm Thursday afternoon, Jackie Cooper was lazing around at home after a busy day at work. As she'd walked past a bookshop window earlier in the week, she was drawn to a specific book on show, *Angel without Wings*; she promptly bought it and took it home. She couldn't put the book down, but eventually her eyes began to feel heavy and droop, and the words became blurry.

The sky was turning beautiful colors each evening as the sun began to set behind the distant mountains. The once warm breeze had cooled. Reading *Angel without Wings* was soon an afternoon routine, and after getting home, Jackie would sit in her favorite lounger in the yard and soak up the sun.

Tonight as she reached for her drink on the table beside her, she looked up to see which of the stars would be first to blink into view. The tail of a shooting star caught her eye, streaking across the blue before it apparently stopped. But then it seemed to be getting

1

larger. Dumbfounded, she had no time to move before the shooting star smacked her on the forehead.

When Jackie awoke, the sun had set completely. It was dark, cold, and silent. She was sprawled on the grass, dazed. She gazed up at the stars. Her head throbbed with a nasty headache. *I can't believe that meteor hit me!*

After forcing herself to sit up, she rubbed her forehead and felt a large and painful bump. *I must have been out for a good few hours,* she thought.

Jackie saw a glowing black-and-silver rock on the ground next to her. It was making a low humming sound. Warily, she left the rock alone, got to her feet, and went inside.

She stood in front of the closet mirror and looked herself over, peering at her forehead. Nothing looked amiss. Puzzled, she lifted her hand and touched the large bump that was obviously there. How could she feel a painful bump on her forehead but look normal in the mirror reflection? *Why can't I see the bump on my head?*

She had been an astrophysicist for six years. She knew how hot meteorites should not be touched, which was why she'd left that one alone. But how was she still alive? Being hit by a meteorite should have meant a one-way trip to the morgue.

She should call the office and explain what happened, but that would bring lots of probing questions. How was she supposed to answer when they asked why she wasn't dead?

She went into the kitchen, made herself a hot tea, and sat down. As she took a sip, she thought about the situation she found herself in: alone in her home. Then she started thinking back to when she was studying.

At university, Jackie was three years younger than her classmates because she had graduated high school early. In the last year of her master's degree, she was voted the student most likely to succeed and given the title Miss Southern University Beautiful Belle from four different universities in the state. Her long, jet black hair and her strikingly beautiful features had made her the town's Miss Killeen in all the beauty contests for the past ten years, which she was quite proud of.

She kept fit by running a couple of miles nearly every morning, having a healthy breakfast, and going to the gym twice a week, before working at the Institute of Space Studies in Austin, Texas. She left early to drive the seventy-odd miles from her home just outside Killeen. This was originally her dad's second home; Jonathan Cooper gave it to her after she graduated university. She loved the peace and quiet it provided, especially as there were no neighbors for miles around. At night, she spent her time looking at the stars through her Celestron telescope, which she'd set up in an observatory in the backyard.

About an hour after Jackie got home, at the water tower approximately half a mile away, scruffy Billy Barnes sat on his pickup truck. The sheriff's son, he was a clever young man who had started his own business renovating and customizing old cars. His customers came from near and far and were always lining up for his work.

About two years ago, still healthy, he was walking home with his mom one afternoon, while helping her with the shopping. It had been a warm, dry day, and when Billy learned that she needed help, he would always drop everything to help her. As they were crossing the road, both got knocked down by a hit-and-run drunk driver. The pickup came out of nowhere and then sped off, hitting a few cars on the way out of town. Billy was badly hurt with head injuries, and his mother was killed outright. After that, his life changed dramatically. He had a new nickname in town—"Brainless"—and Jackie, who was his girlfriend, could not cope with his mood swings and drinking. She left him, although they remained friends.

So late Thursday afternoons, like clockwork, Billy was behind the water tower, sitting on the roof or inside of his old pickup truck, depending on the weather. He had his cold beers and cold burger on the seat and a pair of binoculars to spy on Jackie. He still liked her.

This Thursday afternoon, he was looking at Jackie as usual, and soon he was drunk from the beers because the weather was so hot. Through the binoculars, he saw her look up, so he looked up too. A small meteor going across the sky suddenly turned, descended toward her, and then hit her on the head.

"Oh my God!" he shouted as he spat out a mouthful of beer. He panicked. Sliding off the roof, he said to himself, *What to do? What to do? If I rush into town and tell people what happened, they won't believe me and will laugh at me.*

Billy decided to go help Jackie himself.

He jumped into the truck and tried to start up the engine, with no success. He banged the steering wheel.

"Come on, you hunk of junk!" But for all he tried, his truck was dead. It would not start.

He got out of the truck and stumbled drunkenly toward Jackie's home. But he did not see the water tower frame and ran into it, knocking himself out.

Jackie decided to go to bed, as she had a bad headache from being hit. For a few hours, she tried to get some sleep, but the pain was getting more intense by the minute, especially on her forehead. She thought, *That rock will need to be examined, but I'll do it in the morning. It won't go anywhere.*

As she lay back again and her head touched the pillow, she fell asleep.

Still a bit dazed, Jackie opened her eyes. Everything at first was a blur, the bump right in the middle of her forehead felt large and painful, and she was hungry. Then she focused on the wall clock. It was still very early, and the morning sun was just starting to shine through the cracks in her curtains.

As she looked around her room, one beam of light struck the bedside table. She was shocked to see the meteor, about the size of a fist, on the table.

"How did that get there?" she asked aloud.

She stood up, still feeling a throbbing from her head. She dressed and then sat on the bed by the table to have a closer look at the rock. She picked up a pencil to poke it, but before she could do that, the rock floated off the table and hovered there.

Okay, she thought. In a loud voice, she said, "Hey, is this some kind of joke?" as she looked around for her workmates to come into the room. But no one came. The house was silent.

So her focus went back to the rock, which settled back onto the table. Being a scientist, she knew better than to touch it, but something was telling her it was safe to pick up. Jackie reached out to the rock, but it moved faster than she did and appeared in her hand before she could move out of the way.

As she touched the rock, a feeling of peace came over her.

Now both hands were holding the rock. Jackie started moving it around and around in her hands. It looked and felt sharp in texture, but there were no sharp edges to it. The rock weighed less than she had imagined. She should know. She had the bump to prove it!

Then it started glowing in her hand, which brought warmth into her hands—as well as a chill. To Jackie's mind, no such thing should exist, yet she was holding the very evidence that proved it did.

Something told her to open her hands. The rock rose and hovered above them. She felt she should close her eyes. The rock started to make that humming sound again, which made Jackie open her eyes to see what was happening. A small ray of light emitted from the rock and touched her on the forehead.

The rock again settled on the table. She felt no pain after the light touched her; it was as if the light soothed away her pain. She got up to make tea and paused by the mirror in the hall. She took a quick look at her hair and then at her brow. Shocked, she rubbed her eyes and peered at her reflection. Her hand went to her forehead and found no bump, nothing out of order.

But now she saw in her reflection what could only be described as a closed third eye.

She went to the kitchen, still touching her head in disbelief. After what seemed hours but was only minutes, she stopped worrying about her head, she decided to go into town despite the early hour; she wanted to see if anyone was awake who might have seen or heard anything during the night. She finished her tea, took one last look in the mirror, and went outside.

CHAPTER 2

Wings of an Angel

As Jackie climbed into the car, she suddenly felt sharp pains in her back, two to be precise: one on each side, near her shoulder blades. The pain was like getting stabbed in the back; and it got more intense as she sat and leaned back onto the car seats. What was going on? She had never had backache before. She opened the door, got out of the car, and stood there for a minute. Her back felt as if it was being torn into two halves. She started shaking her arms and shoulders to try and get rid of the pain.

The pain was growing worse, so she stumbled back to the house. As she reached the porch, overcome, she screamed and collapsed unconscious. When she came to, the pain had gone, so she tried to turn over. But she was covered with a blanket of feathers, which stopped her from rolling over.

She turned her head to see the rock lying beside her. "This all started when you hit me," she said, and the rock glowed as if to reply. Jackie pulled herself onto her

8

knees and held on to the porch rail. She tried to remove the blanket but grabbed instead what resembled a very large bird's wing.

She managed to get inside the house. Feeling very heavy with the blanket on her back, she went into her bedroom and dropped onto the bed. As she relaxed, the phone beside the bed rang. "Jackie, are you okay?" the caller asked. "Are you coming in to work? You are late; that's not like you."

Jackie apologized and said she had woken up with the most terrible headache. *That is no lie*, she thought to herself. She told the caller she would be in early on Monday and hung up. She rose from the bed but still had the blanket on her. She moved to the mirror and stood there in shock and wonderment. She saw the reflection of the bedside table. The rock sitting on it looked back at her reflection, and standing there was Jackie with two silvery-white wings on her back. She turned to one side and reached back to grab hold and pull. *"Ouch!* What? They are attached!" *This has got to be a joke.* She thinks about how her dad would react to his daughter having wings.

She closed her eyes and wondered what to do next. An idea popped into her head: *Just try to move them. Go on; move them*, so she closed her eyes to concentrate. They felt strange because it was like moving another pair of arms but a lot bigger. Now they had stirred a draft in the room as they slowly moved up and down. The third eye on her forehead slowly opened, and at first what Jackie saw was darkness. As more light came in, and she focused, whatever she looked at seemed to be under x-ray vision but in color. She could also see through the walls. She looked up and could see the sky right there, as if her home had no roof. She closed her third eye and opened her eyes.

Next problem she thought: *How will I be able to dress with these wings?* A little voice told her not to worry. She went outside and looked around to make sure no one was there, closed her eyes, opened her third eye, and looked around again. She saw the lights of a truck at the water tower. Looking closer with her new vision, she saw someone on the ground; Billy was lying there. She moved her wings up and down, faster and faster, and off she went. *"Wow,"* she said out loud without thinking. Her liftoff was not too bad, but flying toward the water tower, she was spinning out of control and getting faster, before she realized she was there.

A rough first landing brought her crashing to the ground by Billy's pickup but still moving forward. She nearly knocked herself out on the side of his truck. *Wings away and eyes open*, she thought quickly as she bent to see if he was okay. He had a nasty gash on his head and had been drinking, as his breath and the bottles nearby told her. It looked as if he had been lying there all night, fast asleep.

After getting him into the truck, she started it up easily and drove into town straight to the doctors. Billy woke, mumbling something about Jackie being hurt and needing to help her. The sheriff, his father, had been called and now stood over Billy as he lay on the doctor's couch. He said, "I'm a bit disappointed in you. I thought you were more sensible and had stopped the drinking."

Jackie left after making sure Billy was okay and

started walking up the road toward her house. The sheriff pulled up next to her and asked her if he could give her a lift home. "Yes, that would be good; thanks," and got in the car.

"Thanks for bringing Billy home. My son was a good boy, but since the accident and his mom passing the way she did, I cannot seem to do anything right for him."

Jackie said, "Billy was blaming himself for that, and he's counting on you to find the car and driver that hit them."

"I am trying my best to find that car, but it has disappeared off the face of the earth," the sheriff answered as he pulled into Jackie's drive and stopped just outside the house.

"Thanks, Bill." She laid a hand on his arm. "He will be okay; just give him some time."

As Bill drove off, he shouted back, "He still loves you, you know."

Jackie thought, *I know he does, but he is not the same since the accident*. She went inside and sat in her bedroom, thinking about events of the last few hours. She looked at the rock, and it started to glow. *I wish you could talk to me and tell me what the hell is going on*, and the rock glowed a bit brighter.

Then it started flashing. *Not talk. I can use telepathy to communicate*. Now this was almost too much. She jumped up and moved away, backing up to the wall. *Do not be afraid. I mean you no harm. I have come to you for a reason.*

"Okay, this is getting weird," she said out loud and looked around the room. Then the rock began to vibrate and glow brightly. She was stunned to see it begin to grow and start to take the shape of what looked like a human. Then a young girl aged about fourteen stood before Jackie. She had long black hair and slender features, but there was a strength about her that you would not argue with.

She said, "Jackie, I have taken this form so you will recognize that I am you as a child."

Jackie, shocked, went to the drinks cupboard and poured a large whiskey. But before she could drink it, the glass and its contents vanished.

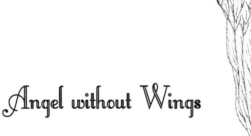

CHAPTER 3

Angel without Wings

"Please sit down and let me explain—please, sit! My name is Reial, and I am your guardian angel. I have been with you since your spirit became a being on this world. I was sent to you by the ascended master to help you find your way. I am to guide you so that strength will come to you when you start helping others. I also need your help in finding a lost soul, because I am here for this quest for one lunar cycle, what you would call twenty-eight days."

Jackie, sitting on her bed, was more stunned the more she heard. "Okay. Let's say I believe you; how can I help an angel? After all, you must have powers to do about anything."

"We are given certain abilities, and when you ask your angel for help, we give it in the best way we can to be the most help. But coming into this plane, we need help, so we ask our physical being friends for help in physical matters." Jackie nodded in understanding.

"We have given you some gifts that you can control

yourself, but they are not visible to others, and they are best used at night."

"Yes, thanks. I've seen and used a couple of them already. Next time try to give me some warning, or tell me what you have planned, okay?"

Jackie decided she'd better get some sleep and asked Reial not to disturb her for a few hours. While lying down, she realized that all her pain was completely gone, and her body felt normal now.

A few hours later she emerged from her room and went looking for Reial. She found her sitting on the porch chair. "So when do we start looking for your lost soul?" she asked.

You have to practice flying and get reliant on using your third eye first, she heard in her head. *I will be talking to you through ESP from now on unless it is vital that I speak.*

Jackie nodded. *Do you eat food or drink?* Just as Jackie was thinking that and Reial was about to answer, a car was pulling up the drive. "Oh no, it's my dad."

After parking and getting out of the car, he waved and said, "Hello, sweet pea. Are you okay?"

"Yes, Dad. What brings you out here?"

Sweet pea!

Jackie looked at Reial: *QUIET!*

"Well I got a call from Bill. He said Billy saw you get hit by a meteorite."

"He had been drinking a lot, and he knocked himself out over by the water tower," Jackie replied.

"How did you know he was there? It's such a long way away."

Thinking quickly, she said, "I saw his truck lights on. I went over to see what was going on and found him."

Dad nodded as if in agreement with that and then said, "And who is this young lady sitting on the porch with you?"

Jackie could have died with shock at that question. She wouldn't have imagined that anyone could see Reial but her. "Um, this is Reial, the daughter of one of my neighbors. She comes over on her bike after school every couple of days because she is interested in the universe. Reial, this is my dad, Jonathan Cooper."

"Pleased to meet you," Reial said. Jackie glanced at her and heard, *This is vital*, as she smiled. "I just love your daughter's observatory, so she lets me look at the stars."

"I suppose you want to fly into space when you are older?" Jackie's dad asked.

"Well, yes, of course," Reial replied. She smiled at Jackie. *I do that already!*

"Um, do you want a drink Dad?" Changing the subject, Jackie turned to go inside. She looked at Reial: *Don't encourage him please, or he will stay here for hours.*

"No, thanks, honey. I've got to go back to work; staying late today. Just popped over to make sure you're okay." With that he blew a kiss, returned to his car, and drove off.

"Well, I never saw that before: Dad coming over and not staying." Jackie turned to Reial. "Say, did you do that?"

Reial just smiled and watched the car going off in the distance. "Yes, please, love something to eat."

Later, the night was dark and clear. Jackie went

outside; it was time to practice her flying and using her third eye. Reial told her to exercise first by closing her eyes and opening her third eye; then she should slowly unfold her wings and stretch them out. Jackie was surprised how wide they spread—at least eighteen feet. Then she started slowly moving them up and down; then she tried it faster. Looking up, she did not feel herself leaving the ground as she rose upward. Then *whoosh*—she was gone, straight up.

Reial stood by the door as the dust settled after that takeoff and smiled. *Perfect,* she thought.

As Jackie quietly landed in control back in front of the house, Reial was waiting for her. *Followed you all the way; that was very good.*

"Thanks, but I need some goggles or glasses to stop my eye from watering. How would that work, is it a gog or glass for one eye?" Jackie laughed.

Reial just looked at her, turned and walked inside. A minute later she came back smiling with what looked like a pirate's patch attached to a woolly hat. *Try this.*

Is this for the joke thing? "Well I thought it was funny," Jackie mumbled.

No. Reial looked at Jackie's hair. *You have a few icicles on your hair as well as your eye running.*

Jackie brushed off her hair, put on the hat, and went up again. She spent a while flying around to get used to the wings and soon felt at home. The view was spectacular as she glided round in circles and came back to earth. As she landed and looked up, she saw Reial sitting on the porch looking very worried. Jackie went over to her and said, "Sorry I was gone so long. Are you okay?"

16

"No. There is something I must tell you about the lost soul we have to find, and I just found out that it's personal to you. I had a visit from ... you would call him my boss, and he told me who we are going to be looking for." Reial gazed into Jackie's eyes. "There is no easy way for me to say this. We will be looking for your mother."

Jackie sat down shocked. She felt anger as memories of her absent mom returned, and then she went deep in thought of all the loving times her dad had gone through. A tear rolled down her cheek.

"Why would anyone want to find a mother who took herself off without caring about the family she left behind?" *Why would I, why would anyone want to do that?*

When Jackie was twelve, Connie Cooper went shopping one day and never came home. The police were informed, and then they found her car in a suburb north of Austin. But after looking for months, they finally admitted they had no clues as to what had happened to her and stopped the search. Jackie's dad then started going out every day for weeks, looking where he could. Then one day he just stopped and carried on living. Still, it broke his heart. Every night she could hear him crying about this till she heard him cry no more.

Now twenty-eight Jackie had almost forgotten her mother. She wanted to forget her for not calling to inquire how she was or what her husband might have gone through. It had been sixteen years. Why should she help with this and what would her dad think?

After some thought, Jackie said to Reial, "Why would you...? Why would your boss want me to do this?

She has not been seen for years. She does not want to be found; otherwise she would have come home by now."

After a pause Reial said, "First let me talk to my boss. I'll be back soon," and she promptly disappeared.

As Jackie sat on the porch waiting she looked up into the sky and saw a shooting star. She made a wish: *I wish I wish upon that star to find my mom come home from afar.* It somehow did not make sense, but it would have to do.

Then Reial appeared and sat down next to Jackie. "The natural order of this life has been disrupted, and it's got to be put back in order. By your mom not coming home, the timeline that should have existed has been changed, and other timelines and lives have altered."

"So are you telling me that the last sixteen years should not have happened?"

"Yes, pretty much," Reial said in a quieter voice.

"Well then, can you tell me why this mix-up happened? How could all this happen?" Jackie asked, getting annoyed and angry.

First calm down. I will explain everything this way so you will understand it quicker. Your mom disappearing had nothing to do with the Spirit. Her energy is still being felt in this galaxy but not in this time, do you understand? We have to find out what has happened and correct this anomaly, and things will get back to normal, but we do not have long.

Okay, but what will happen to the last sixteen years? Jackie asked in a much calmer mind.

"Everything will correct itself over a short time, and at night, too, time will change so as not to upset people. Some of it will seem like a dream and most of it will change without notice. The only person who will know

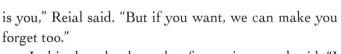

is you," Reial said. "But if you want, we can make you forget too."

Jackie thought about that for a minute and said, "I think I would like to remember both if that's okay."

"We will go out first thing in the morning. Now it's time for bed and sleep."

As Jackie's head hit the pillow, she took a deep breath and blew out a sigh of relief. She had time to think about the situation, and after coming to terms with whom she had to find, she wondered where they would have to start and decided just to get some sleep. While she lay there, her thoughts went back to when her mom was at home and how happy the family was, how much love there was between them, how her Mom helped with her homework. She taught Jackie to cook and sew, which plants were weeds and which were not, and how happy her dad was before Mom disappeared. She closed her eyes with tears running down her face and finally went to sleep.

Billy Barnes

ill Barnes had a hard life, but he was not a hard man. His wife and son were his life, and he wanted the town to be as good as it could be for his family and the other families. So he applied for the job of sheriff of Killeen; their last sheriff had retired, and no one else had stood up for that task.

The year before the family moved to Killeen from LA, Bill was a sergeant in the force there but was getting disillusioned. He sensed a lack of commitment and respect in the unit, and the violence was getting worse on the streets with no one doing anything about it. So he moved back to Killeen with Martha, his wife. This was the city where his own dad had been born and raised, where Bill was born, and where he'd met Martha. Some of his friends knew that he'd been in the police, so they asked him to apply for the job as sheriff. He landed it without much trouble.

Billy was six years old when his dad became sheriff and as he grew up, he became more and more interested in old vintage cars. He started to drive his mom crazy when after his sixteenth birthday his dad brought him the oldest truck in the city and told him to fix it; that was the only car he would buy him. But this lad was going to show everyone that he could make the pile of junk in the yard work. Billy started bringing parts of the car into the house to clean, and that was when his mom started shouting at him about the mess. So he was made to use the old barn for all his car parts.

Billy was a smart young man and did well in school. He always looked well dressed, and all the young girls were always trying to get him to take them out, but his only interest was his cars. Until, that is, a new family moved into the area. Their daughter, Jackie, started at school and was put into some of the same classes as Billy. In the blink of an eye he lost interest in cars. When they first met, he asked her out, and they went on their first date.

It was love for Billy and Jackie, but she told him to carry on with his cars because he was getting so good at repairing them that he was now earning money from doing repairs. Before long his dad suggested they both put up a new barn so Billy could work in it while still in school and then start up his business. So he went on to college and did a business degree to help start and grow his car repair passion.

From the start his business thrived, and he had lots of customers coming from near and far for his work on engines, body repairs, and building; he was a natural.

He had to start employing extra help, and soon the business was getting too big for one building, so he had another one built next to the barn he was using. It was much larger and built of brick.

Billy and Jackie had been dating a while and everyone expected them to get married, His business had taken off in a big way, and he was always working. Jackie went to university and got a master's degree in astrophysics and started working at the Institute for Space Studies in Austin, Texas. They were always together when they had free time, the perfect couple in everyone's eyes.

Bill had been sheriff for twelve years now and he was still relatively young for a sheriff; the last had retired in his early sixties. Bill still had ten years or so to work and keep his town quiet. Over the last two years freeways were being built near the town, and this made the small place bigger as larger roads were joining towns with better access to the whole state. So now Bill's job had got a lot busier due to the larger population in the town and the more routes in and out to patrol.

Bill would drive his wife, Martha, into town to do the shopping, wait for her to finish, and drive her home again. One day he got called away, so that left Martha in town shopping. She called Billy, and he came in and helped her. But then, while they were crossing the road to get back to Billy's truck, a motorist sped around the corner, hit both Billy and his mom, stopped, and then sped away, hitting a few cars on the way out of town. Witnesses later told the sheriff that the driver looked drunk and very scruffy and had a beard.

The hit-and-run killed Martha and affected Billy's brain from the blow to his head when he landed. Within months he lost his business, Jackie stopped seeing him, and he became the town drunk. He was untidy, had grown a beard and was driving his old banged-up truck again.

On the second anniversary of his mom's death, Billy got really drunk. He left the bar and took a truck from the parking lot. He then started driving around in a crazy state, going through red lights and colliding with a parked car. He could barely see what he was doing.

As he drove under the freeway, he went through an energy vortex. This was while a portal was open, taking people into it, and this sent the truck into the past, which Billy did not know. The flash of light as he went through blinded him. He then drove back into town to return the truck but was going too fast and lost control. As he rounded a corner, he did not brake enough and hit two people crossing the road.

Drunk as he was, he could not even focus on who it was he had hit. He stopped for a moment to try and see who they were but then drove off at speed, hitting more cars on the way out of town. He never realized that he had in fact collided with himself and his mom. Then he went back to Austin and drove back through the same energy vortex, again without a clue, bringing him back to his own time.

As Billy sat in the truck back at the bar's parking lot, he tried to visualize the two people that he'd hit, but they weren't clear. And how come it was dark after he'd left the bar, then daylight after he drove around, and then dark again the next minute? While trying to think about what had just happened, Billy suddenly felt very tired. He had to sleep, as he was very confused. So he got out of the truck and, stumbling along, managed to find his own truck, got in, and promptly fell asleep in the front seat.

After hours of sleep, it was now very early in the morning. Billy started waking up, headachy from his drinking bout the night before, with the print of the seat design on the side of his face. He didn't know where he was and had no recall of what happened the night before. All he knew was that he had a blinding hangover and was very thirsty and hungry. Looking around, he saw no shops that would be open this early, so he started his truck and headed home.

As he passed some parked cars and trucks, he saw one with some damage to the front fender and hood but took no notice, as he couldn't remember anything about last night. He drove home carefully and parked by the new barn that was his workshop; his dad kept it locked because of all the tools that were now stored in there. He got out, gazed at the building, and wiped the dust off the window to look inside. He bowed his head and set off to the house. A few tears rolled down his cheek as he tried to remember the past, but it had long gone now. He wished that things could be as they were five years ago, when he could remember all that went on in his life and his mom was standing by the kitchen window waving. He gulped a tall glass of water, stumbled to his bed, and collapsed across it into oblivion.

His dad was shouting from the kitchen, "If you don't come down for your breakfast, I will throw it out."

Billy sat up in bed, his head pounding just a little now. He got dressed and was soon downstairs sitting at the table with his dad. He drank his juice down in one gulp, as he was still thirsty, and proceeded to eat his breakfast.

Bill looked at him and said, "Were you out late drinking again? You always look a mess these days. Smarten yourself up today and have a shave. We are going to see your mom, okay?"

Billy nodded and carried on eating. His dad stood up, already in his uniform looking very smart. He headed toward the door and stopped at the mirror to put his hat on. He turned back and said, "I will be back for you at noon. You be ready—and have a shower; you smell of alcohol."

At a quarter past twelve, Bill and Billy were standing at the side of Martha's grave. It had been two years now, and still no one had a clue who'd been driving that truck.

CHAPTER 5

The First Sparkle

When Jonathan Cooper left university with his master's degree in physics, astrophysics, cosmology, and space exploration, the initials after his name were MPhys.DIS, which left him just short of being a professor. Not that he was short; he was six foot four, and his daughter was looking to be a tall lady too.

He was one of the top scientists at the Institute, working on space products for exploring the universe. Connie, Jackie's mom, met Jonathan at university, and they started in the same study group and worked on the same projects just to be together. After university they moved to Austin to be near the Institute for Space Studies, where they were both employed.

A year after getting married and moving into their first house, Connie had her first child; they named him Nathan. She began working only part time at the Institute while looking after Nathan. Then she had Jackie about eighteen months later and left work completely to raise the children.

Their house was just outside Austin, in a quiet suburb with a spacious yard for the children to play in. Jonathan converted part of the loft space to install an observatory. Most Sundays he would work there, and then in the evenings he and Jackie would be looking up at the sky trying to count all the stars.

As a child Jackie was the smartest girl in the school. Her brother was also very smart but was into sports and loved swimming. On Nathan's twelfth birthday his dad got him professional swimming lessons for a whole year at the local swimming pool and would drive him there and back. Nathan soon became one of the best swimmers in Texas, representing his home and county in national swimming contests.

Every evening after supper, as the sun started to set, they would all go outside and lie down on a ground blanket to look up at the stars. Dad started a game when the kids first started talking, which they all enjoyed playing together. He called it "the first sparkle," and the child who saw the first star in the evening sky got to stay up one hour later with Dad on the blanket watching the stars. It was fun while the kids were young, but then Nathan in his early teens started to go out with his school friends, bike riding then skateboarding at the local park; then it was young crushes on the girls in class.

While Jackie wanted to learn more about the stars and their names, Dad started working later on important projects for the government from the Institute. So Mom started showing young Jackie how to cook and sew and how to grow flowers and food in the garden. Then she would sit with her in the evenings and teach her all about the stars and their names, which Jackie then memorized. On her twelfth birthday, sitting with her mom, Jackie spotted the first star of the evening. Mom asked her to make a quiet wish for anything she most wanted in her young life, so she closed her eyes and made a wish.

A few weeks after that wish, while Jackie was at school, Connie got ready to go shopping. She wanted to go into Austin to look for a telescope for Jackie's birthday. She had talked to Jonathan about that, and he agreed that she could look, and then they'd go in together to get one. With her shopping bags on the passenger seat, she started off. It was a bright, clear afternoon, and ahead the sky was getting a few dark clouds but nothing to worry about.

Going under the freeway where the new flyover had been built, Connie stopped at a stop signal. Looking around as you do, she caught a glimpse of light just under the bridge and thought it looked like someone lying on the ground with an arm waving. She decided to park and try to help.

Just beyond the stoplights she pulled into a small parking lot and walked back across the street. As she got to where she'd seen the light just under the flyover, the light grew stronger, and she saw one or two figures standing in the light. She called out to them, and they said, "If you want to live without fear, come over to us."

Connie was not convinced about what was going on and turned to walk away. But the light reached out, and in the next instant no one was standing under the bridge.

CHAPTER 6

Mr. Atos

The next morning Jackie sat up in bed for some time, listening to the sounds outside but deep in thought about the day her mom had left. It had been raining that morning, but the sun had also come out, trying to break up the clouds. There was a double rainbow, which made one half of the sky quite bright and the other dark. Jackie remembered this because it was very unusual to see a double rainbow; she had said that to her mom, who agreed with her.

Later her mom said she was going into Austin shopping. She gathered up her shopping bags and drove away, even though she was not keen on driving that large car. The car was found on the outskirts of Austin, which was strange because Mom would not have stopped there; the shopping malls were a good distance away, and she would not have been able to walk that far.

After some time, the police stopped looking for Connie, with the excuse that no sign of her had been found. They told the family she'd probably gone to stay with relatives. So Jackie's dad started going out every day after work, driving around to search. He would came home late each evening, sit down with Jackie, and go through where he had been, where he'd started from and where he'd finished. He always became very emotional and cried in Jackie's arms, but it became a ritual.

Jackie had not forgotten and just put the memory away into the back of her mind, but now it was time to remember again. She decided to start where her mom's car was found and try to find a trail from there, even if it was a small one. After having breakfast, she and Reial decided to drive to the outskirts of Austin to the small parking lot. After arriving and parking at the back of the lot, Jackie sat there for a moment and closed her eyes, trying to get a feel of what had been going through her mom's head.

Then Jackie and Reial both got out and took a look around. On this side of the main road the lot did not have many parking spaces. It had a few trees for shade and a few shrubs on islands dividing up the parking bays. The small building in the center of the lot was a local bank, and usually they had a few parking spaces around them.

On the other side of the road was a larger parking lot, which backed up to the freeway, larger stores, and the overhead flyover feeding downtown traffic. Her mom must have driven up to and come under the freeway to the stoplights, crossed the main road, and turned into this parking lot. Why? Had she seen someone she knew, or had something distracted her? Why did she park in this particular spot? She didn't even have an account at this bank.

Turning to Reial, Jackie said, "Let's walk back across

the road and go under the freeway bridge. Let's visualize driving to the parking lot from the other side, okay?"

Reial nodded, and both headed off to the crossing. As they got to the underpass and started to go under the freeway, Reial started to feel dizzy, gripped Jackie's arm and nearly collapsed. Jackie helped her walk past the bridge to the junction where the busy roads met. Once there, Reial seemed to be her normal self, but she turned to Jackie and said, "There is something not of this world giving off energy under that bridge, and it's affecting the normal space and time. That must be why I felt as if I'd lost my way."

They both carefully headed back to the car. Just before the freeway, Jackie stopped and pulled Reial back. "Wait; I'm just going to try something." Jackie closed her eyes, opened her third eye, and looked at the freeway. In that moment she saw what seemed to be a dark energy vortex with a white light core. It emerged from a hole in the concrete under the freeway, which looked like a portal going through to another place or time or even another dimension. On this side of the concrete by the hole were markings. She tried to memorize them.

Jackie stepped back, closed her third eye, and opened her eyes. She became aware of Reial pulling at her arm. All the time she'd been looking at the portal, Reial had been trying to pull her away, as if she was being drawn into the energy vortex. Two whole hours had passed.

On their way back to the car, they both had to pass under the freeway, where Reial fainted. Jackie had to carry her back to the parking lot.

Reial awoke as they got back to the car. Jackie said, "I have to look again and see if there are any markings on the wall on this side."

"What markings?" Reial asked, rousing. "Did you see some on the wall with your open eye? Can you remember them or describe them? In fact, try to draw them now before you forget." She reached into the car and brought out a piece of paper and a pencil. Jackie drew the symbols that she'd seen and handed the paper to Reial.

She studied them for a while. Then she looked up at Jackie. *These symbols open a doorway to the lower realms, and someone has seen them and read them out loud to open this vortex, either on purpose or by accident. The vortex cannot be opened from the other place unless there is a half kin walking around. We must go home now!*

After arriving back home, Jackie and Reial both sat on the porch for a while in silence. They were so deep in thought that they did not notice the appearance of a tall, dark figure standing at the end of the drive looking at them. Reial was the first to notice him and firmly took Jackie's hand. *Do not say a word. I will talk for both of us, okay?* Jackie nodded.

As the figure approached, they saw he was mysteriously dressed all in black, with a wide-brimmed black hat. He had a long, thin face and sharp cheekbones, deep eyes, and a pale complexion. His arms hung out of his long coat sleeves and had slender long fingers. His black coat hung to the tops of his slim black shoes that tapered to long points.

As he walked up the dusty drive, he left no prints in the dry dirt as if he were walking just above the ground. "Good day to you," the stranger said to the girls, touching his hat.

"What can I help you with?" Reial said abruptly, standing up.

"You must be Reial. I have heard a lot about you." Then, looking at Jackie, he said, "And you must be the new fledgling, Jackie. How goes the flying practice?"

Without waiting for her answer, he looked back at Reial and came to the point, almost shouting. "If you interfere in matters that do not concern you, there will be consequences."

Reial lifted her arm, pointed a finger upward, said, "Hold that thought," and promptly vanished.

Within what seemed like minutes she reappeared, looking quite serious and was about to talk when Jackie addressed her silently: *Reial, who is this man, and where did you go, leaving me alone with this bonehead?*

"She went to her boss, and I am not a bonehead!" said the stranger, as he looked right into Jackie's eyes. *Thoughts are very powerful if you use them correctly. Isn't that right, Reial?*

Reial turned to Jackie and asked her to keep her thoughts to herself and to please be quiet. Then she stepped off the porch and turned back to the stranger.

"Now first of all, Mr. Atos, you should not be in this realm, and you do not have any say or power here because this is my side." Reial said.

She began to grow and was soon a head taller than Mr. Atos. Her wings unfolding and spread wide open, a pure white so bright that even Mr. Atos stepped back and covered his eyes.

Jackie covered her eyes too but not before she saw the amazing transformation of Reial into the most beautiful creature she had ever seen. Standing very tall and hovering about a foot off the ground with a twelve to fourteen-foot wingspan, the feathers beautifully iridescent, almost clear but with hints of sparkly color, she was dressed in shimmering silver that looked like armor, with a very large sword at her side, a pure white being—the angel within Reial.

"This is the only warning you will get. Leave this place, *now!*" The voice was so strong that it shook the porch and the ground. As quickly as Mr. Atos had arrived, he was gone. *Wow!* Was Jackie's thought; *please remind me not to get you annoyed.*

Reial turned to her. *I am sorry, but that is the only way to get rid of demons, and he is the worst.* As she calmed down, she slowly changed back. The light slowly dimmed and her wings simply folded and faded away, finally she was the young girl again. She stepped back onto the porch and sat by Jackie as if nothing had happened.

"Do you know that you rock? You just kicked serious butt there, and the size of your wings was simply humongous. OMG, you are so beautiful." With that Jackie gave her a big, warm hug and started crying.

Reial was the first to talk after a long silence. "Let's get some sleep for a couple of hours. Then we'll eat, and then we'll get Mom back, okay?"

"Sounds like a great plan." They both went inside and then there was silence from the house.

A few hours later the light went on in Jackie's room. Sitting on the side of the bed and dressed, she remembered looking at the table and seeing the rock; she recalled it humming to her. But the rock was not there now.

There was a knock at the door. *Are you ready? I have made you something to eat.*

Thanks; I will be right out.

After eating, they both got into the car and sat there for a while in silence. Jackie started the car but then turned to Reial and was about to speak when a thought came into her head. *What if, when we get to where we're going and find your mom, we can't get back? How will we explain what happened to the others?*

After a thoughtful pause, Jackie drove off into the fading light. *If we cannot come back, we won't need to explain to anyone, will we?*

Reial nodded back in agreement and smiled.

It had started off as a clear evening like the last few, but suddenly, within a few minutes, very dark clouds covered the whole sky, which made it look later than it was. The rain started as they got to the freeway. They stopped at the stoplights just past the parking lot. Suddenly, lightning blanketed the whole sky, with a blast of thunder that shook the car.

As they passed under the bridge, lightning again lit up the sky but this time directly over the freeway. The thunder seemed to shake the whole world. Some moments later, although a few cars still stood in the parking lot, no cars came under the freeway bridge—and there was no sign of Jackie or Reial or their car. Everything was quiet once more; the clouds were gone, and the night sky blazed with stars.

CHAPTER 7

The Portal

The lights had suddenly gone out under the freeway. Jackie stopped the car and looked out through the windshield with the high beams on. She saw nothing but darkness, as if the world had switched off with no clouds, no stars, no lights, and no parking lot. She switched off the lights and tried to focus on what was outside the car. She became aware of small white dots moving around.

Then in the distance she saw a light; it looked like a white flame flickering in the dark. *Someone lit a fire in the middle of the parking lot,* she thought.

Reial said, "We are not in the human world anymore; someone opened the portal doorway and pulled us in."

Jackie grasped what Reial had just said and started to panic. Her breathing sped up, but Reial touched her, and that disappeared. As they sat in the car with the darkness outside, both heard a familiar voice start talking to them. "Well, well. Hello, fledgling, and hello, Reial. I warned you both not to interfere. Now this bonehead has the upper hand, because this is now my domain where I have the power."

The two looked at each other, and Reial said, "Is that what you think, Mr. Atos? If I were to say three words to you now, I wonder what you would do." She slid a hand into her pocket and gripped the rock that was in there. She held it tight, with the words on the tip of her tongue.

"And what three words could you possibly say to me that would make me do anything other than keep you locked up to do my bidding forever?"

"Before I say them, I will ask you this and give you a single chance to answer. Are you going to return everyone back to the reality where they should have remained before you interfered in the Maker's writing of life?"

"I will answer you, but first I want you to see for yourselves what I am doing so that when you join us, you will be able to accept this reality as yours." Then he laughed, and the ground shook. He loudly called, "Light!" A cube of the dark space lit up but not with sunlight—just white light, and it reached ten feet above the heads of figures gathered around. Their eyes were white, but all their clothes, everything about them, and even their features were all black. To find someone in this reality would be hard.

From each person a black connecting cord rose from their head into the black space. The women assumed that was how they were being controlled by Mr. Atos so they had to do whatever they were told. It looked as though each worker was tearing away at the wall that had the portal going through it.

Reial looked at Jackie and whispered, "Can you

see anything else about this place that might help us understand what he is up to?" So Jackie closed her eyes and opened her third eye. This time she did not have x-ray vision but normal vision. She looked around and saw all the people suddenly stop and look at her as if they knew she could see them. Then without a word they went back to what they were doing. As Jackie scanned around, she could see they were trying to break through the wall to the human world. She looked up to the black space and saw hundreds of flying demons ready to go through the portal when it opened. They too suddenly looked at Jackie as if they sensed her observing, and two or three started flying down toward her. She opened her eye quickly and told Reial all she had seen.

Realizing what Mr. Atos was up to, Reial knew she must find Jackie's mom and free all the other humans and take them from this place. Otherwise they would have their souls and energy taken when the breach broke, and then Mr. Atos would turn them into demons. This would not be easy; they must somehow cut all the cords and get everyone through the portal. Then each one would have to be sent back to their homes, and all the timelines must be changed to accept each individual back. First Reial and Jackie had to see how many humans Mr. Atos had taken from their reality and what could be done to stop this attempt at invading the human world with demons.

Deciding that she had to take a look around, Reial told Jackie that she had to go off with Mr. Atos to talk about what was going on and whether they could come to some arrangement to free Jackie's mom. "I want you to find a way of freeing as many people as you can or all of them, and get them ready to go back through the portal. I will keep Mr. Atos busy and then get the portal open."

Jackie nodded and asked, "How do you plan on opening the portal when it will only open from the other side?"

"Have faith, and all will be revealed." She gave Jackie a hug and walked away to find Mr. Atos.

Still sitting in the car Jackie looked around to see what would be effective against darkness and demons. She opened the glove compartment and found a few letters and a flashlight. A flashlight was great for turning dark into light, so she switched it on, shone it on the roof of the car, and switched it off. *It works*, she said to herself—but without realizing that when she switched it on, part of the light came out of the car and cleared some of the black above, freeing two people by cutting their ties to the darkness.

Jackie got out with the flashlight and decided to look in the trunk to see if there was anything she could use. She opened it and had a good look. She found the spare tire, an old car battery with starter cables, a bag with some tools, spare light bulbs for the car, and a large spray can of black tire wall paint. As she pondered what to use, a hand touched her shoulder, which made her jump. She whirled around to object to Reial for frightening her and saw two women standing in front of her. Their faces and clothes looked partially normal in color but still mostly black. Their eyes were normal, but half their faces were blacked out and looking frightened.

One of them asked, "Where are we, please? What is this place, and how did we get here?"

"Don't worry. We will all be safe soon, but I need your help. Please, we have to change all these people back to normal and get them out. How did you become half normal again?"

The same woman answered, "A light came from the car window and touched us, and this happened. It also cut the cords that were controlling us and forcing us to work."

Jackie thought for a moment; clearly, that took place when she switched on the flashlight. Her hopes rose that she could indeed free the people. Then, looking back at the things in the trunk, she had an idea about freeing all the people at once and getting them to the portal. But it must work at the same time as Reial opening the portal.

Next problem was to figure out how Reial would get the portal open and everyone out. *Reial, can you talk— sorry,* think *to me at the moment?*

No, sorry, get back to you soon.

Well, I'm on my own and will have to work everything out with my helpers, thought Jackie.

CHAPTER 8

Black to White

"**L**adies, can you help me by making some holes in this tire?" Jackie counted the bulbs she had and asked them to make six holes in the tire. She began to rig up the starter leads to the bulbs and to the old battery. Then she pushed the bulbs into the holes and connected them to the cable inside the tire. *This ought to work if the battery isn't dead.*

She clipped a cable to one battery terminal and just touched the other two together. The bulbs lit up, so she pulled it off quickly so as not to attract any attention from the demons. Then she looked around to see what the light had done. The ladies were fully colored and back to normal. Some others were partially back with their cords disconnected, and some of the black above them had given way to white.

Then suddenly one of the demons swooped down at Jackie and tried to attack her, but when it reached the white space, it fell to the ground, removing part of its wings.

Then the demon got up and screeched to alert the others flying above, but what came out was "Help!" *This demon is human!* She switched on the flashlight and aimed it at the demon in a short burst of light. Collapsing to the ground it curled up as if in agony, and started to change back into a human. As it stood up, Jackie watched as its clawed arms became arms and hands, its talons became toes; its legs formed, and finally it became a man.

Maybe we can change all the other demons too. Then Mr. Atos will have no way to defend himself. And we will need to change them all at the same time—but how?

After talking with the changed ones, as she began calling them, she decided with them to clear more black space away from the ground area to make the white as large as possible but without getting noticed. She decided to use the black spray to disguise the white space as black.

So moving along with the flashlight to the edge of the black space and one of the women to apply the black spray, Jackie used her light to change the black space to white and making it larger to hold more people as they were changed back. The woman with her sprayed above their heads to make it look as if the whole place was still black space. After what felt like hours, they managed to change a very large area to white space.

Now Jackie had to draw the demons down to the white so she could change them back to their human forms. First she told the changed ones to move away from her. Then she closed her eyes, opened her third eye, and looked up. She saw lots of demons flying around. Then, apparently sensing her, they began descending toward her, but as they got to the white space, they started dropping like flies onto the ground. She switched on the flashlight and shone it on all the fallen demons, and they started changing back to their human form.

Before she knew it, her flashlight was out of power. She called to the women to switch on the power for the tire lights. As they did so, Jackie closed her third eye and opened her eyes to see lots of humans standing in front of her. Still more demons were falling and being changed back to their human forms. All the black space started to change back to white space as more light spread, and more of the humans who were connected to the cords started changing from black to their natural coloring, along with their clothes.

When Reial left Jackie, having told her to find a way to change all the people back to themselves and get them ready to leave, she opened her wings and flew upward passing into the black space. She saw all the demons flying around and realized that Mr. Atos had changed all these too. He was planning to change everyone, but she could not warn Jackie, because then he would know what they were trying to do.

She flew above the black space to an area that had nothing. There she found Mr. Atos sitting on his large black, ornately decorated throne with seven pillars around it and fronted by black marble steps. Two demons stood nearby, looking like guards, but he waved a hand, and they changed back to their human form, one male and the other female. Then he said to Reial, "Is this better for you than demons? The male is called Elfadam and the female Nightglade."

Reial nodded, and as she looked at the female more closely, she recognized her as Jackie's mom, but what was she doing so close to Mr. Atos? A black marble seat rose up from the floor near Reial, and she sat down. She glanced at Connie and saw her eyes seemingly glazed over as if by a spell or a trance.

Suddenly a very large demon flew past, landed just behind Reial, and bowed to Mr. Atos but stood where it was. Mr. Atos looked at the demon with a nod and then turned to Reial. "Why did you come into my realm?"

"I came here"—she paused. "This is not your realm, is it? You took it for your own. What have you done with the beings living here?"

"I have converted them to my way of thinking, and they are now helping me in my endeavor to rule."

"So you have forced them to work for you," Reial said grimly.

"You have no say in what I do in my own domain. I ask again, why did you come into my realm?"

"I came here to get a soul who does not belong in this place. You took this being, and now it has disrupted the flow of time in the human world."

"I did not take anyone who did not come willingly into the portal," said Mr. Atos.

"So how did you tempt anyone into the portal? By offering them immortality? What did you offer them? Maybe they got pulled into your portal by mistake and without you realizing it; that is why you have attracted the attention of the Highest Angel of all. He then went to the Light and was told he must get the lost back to their timelines at any cost." Reial was growing more assertive, trying to make Mr. Atos admit to his mistakes.

Mr. Atos sensed that he had slipped up. He stood and raised his arms, to draw his demons to him, but Reial called out, "Stop! Before you do this, think about all the lives that will be lost and have been lost by you starting your takeover of everything, of time itself!"

"It will be all part of the new order, of me becoming the new God and every creature in the universe becoming my slave." And he again began to call his demons to him.

With that Reial reached into her pocket and took hold of the stone. She pulled it out and held it above her head, and the stone began glowing brightly. Her hand started to glow the same color as the stone, and she exclaimed, "These are the three words that I warned you about," and she said them out loud: "White Angel Orblight."

Suddenly she again became the beautiful angel within, transforming to her largest size yet. The stone had multiplied her power, and impressively before Mr. Atos, Reial the angel of light floated, her wings outstretched twenty feet in each direction.

The bright light pouring from her spread across the black and white space, changing all beings back to their natural forms.

As the black changed back to white, the pillars and Mr. Atos's black throne also changed to white. The large demon flew off and started circling, but the energy did not change it. All the beings around had to hide their eyes from the light; it was so bright that it seemed as if the sun was right there.

Mr. Atos, blinded at first, tried to counter the angel's

light by raising his arms and firing his pure black energy back at her, but that turned to white energy with rainbow highlights when it reached her force, which then turned back at him. This struggle went on for a good hour before Mr. Atos's energy was finally drained dry. He sat down in defeat as everything around him became energized white light.

"That was a very disappointing battle," Reial said sarcastically. "I thought you would have more staying power than that." But she hadn't noticed the large demon coming up behind her. It took a swipe at her hand, going after the stone.

As it grabbed her hand, Mr. Atos stood up and said, "I had to pretend to be weak when there was another way to get what I wanted, and this is what I want: your energy, to make me the greatest God of all time and in every time. I knew He would give you the stone of light to try and defeat me, but I knew that if I made a demon that was not affected by the light, it would get me the stone. Now, Agron, bring me the stone."

Reial tightened her grip on the stone, and the demon had her hand in its claw. She recited a message that her boss told her in case she should find herself in a difficult situation: "Remember that throwing a stone into a pond makes far more ripples than throwing the stone onto hard ground." With that, she opened her hand, and the stone slipped out and fell. The demon could not grip the stone; it was too small for its claws. Mr. Atos reached out to try to catch the falling stone but missed it.

The demon let go of Reial and flew after the stone. So did Reial, but she stopped the demon by grabbing hold of its wings. Then she began to spin, going faster and faster till she let go, throwing the demon upward, away from the falling stone.

The stone hit the ground and sent out a wave of light that turned everything else back to normal that wasn't already white and caused a white mist to cover the whole of the domain. It also started to open the portal. The people could see all the different parts of the world that they had come from, and they now started to leave.

Mr. Atos said, "You tricked me into going for the stone so that you would drop it and change my domain. Very clever." As he now sat, the white energy started to spread up his long black coat. His shoes were now white. His face began to age, and his hair turned white. Soon all of Mr. Atos was white, and everything that was his had again become part of the world of normal beings and angels.

Jackie looked up to see the portal opening and realized that Reial must have beaten Mr. Atos somehow. She knew that she had to help the people go back to their homes. She started telling them to leave through the portal. As she watched them go, each went back to the time and place from which they had entered the portal. When all had gone and it was Jackie's and Reial's turn, they entered the portal holding hands. Reial came back alone, stopped, and smiled.

CHAPTER 9

The Truth

When Jackie opened her eyes, everything was a blur. All she saw were blurred figures standing around her. The pain coming from her head did not help as she tried to focus. Everyone looked fuzzy until at last she recognized her dad. She smiled, and he smiled back.

"Hi, sweet pea. How are you feeling?"

"Hi, Dad." Still confused, she gazed around the room, "I'm okay, but my head hurts. Why am I here?"

Trying to focus a bit more to see who else was in the room, she saw Billy smiling at her. *Why is he smiling at me like that?* Smartly dressed with his neatly combed head of brown hair, he looked as though he'd just been to church. Trying to smile back she then noticed Bill Barnes, the sheriff, talking with Dr. Trent. Their words were indistinguishable; it must be serious if the sheriff was here.

Dr. Trent noticed that she had come around and stepped toward her. He asked her to relax, sit up slowly, and lean forward. Checking her head he proceeded to arrange her pillows so she could sit more upright with back support. He said, "When Billy cycled back into town and told us a meteor had hit you on the head, we all thought the worst. You were badly hurt, but you are one tough young girl." He picked up his clipboard at the foot of the bed. Everyone in the room audibly agreed.

"How long have I been in the hospital? It was only yesterday that we spoke when you came over to the house and met Reial," she said to her dad.

"You have been in the hospital since Billy and the sheriff brought you from our house. That was three days ago, after the accident; you and Billy were both in the yard. Don't you remember" He continued, "I come home every evening after work; we see you every day. And who is Reial? Is she a friend from school?"

He turned to the doctor and quietly asked, "Has she got amnesia or something from the knock to her head?"

Standing in the doorway just behind Billy, Connie was smiling through tears of joy that her baby was safe. Jackie saw her, burst out crying, and stretched her arms toward her mom.

Connie rushed in and sat down on the edge of the bed to give her girl a cuddle. She whispered, "Thank you for saving me and all of us."

In the back of her mind Jackie heard Reial's thoughts: *Hey, did I tell you how good you were! Well, you were, and I am very proud to have worked with you and become your friend.*

Jackie thought back, with an inward smile, *Back at you, but no, not just a friend, my dear sister. Thank you for helping me get my mom back and get everything back to normal. Say, do I have to go back to school too?*

A few days later, when the doctor was confident that Jackie was not concussed or badly injured, just bruised from the blow, they let her go home to the care of her mother. This home was the one she remembered as her mom and dad's. As she stepped into the hall, she looked into the mirror to see a twelve-year-old girl who looked like Reial, an angel who will come to her sixteen years from now to help her get her mom back. A tear rolled down her cheek as she remembered.

Late one afternoon as the sun was going down, Jackie sat outside with her dad, looking up at the sky for the first stars of the evening. "Dad, will you get me a house when I get older and build me an observatory in the back so that I can look up at all the stars at night whenever I want to?"

"You know I will; it's written in the stars." They both laughed and gave each other a hug. "You have been a brave girl, sweet pea, these last few days. I hope that does not stop you doing what you decided a few weeks ago about going to college and university." Then he said in a low voice, so her mom would not hear, "And tell Reial she is welcome anytime."

She looked at her dad in surprise as he winked at her. Then he smiled, got up, and started to go inside. He stopped by the half-opened door, turned, and said, "Don't stay up too late as you have school tomorrow." Then he went on in a stage whisper: "And say good night to Reial for me, sweet pea."

He blew her a kiss and went inside. Jackie sat in

amazement at what had just happened. Her dad somehow knew, but it was a complete mystery to her.

Then the back door opened, and Mom came out and sat next to her. "Dad's gone to bed with a big smile. What were you two talking about? Oh my, what a nice cool evening to sit on the porch. Look, those must be the first stars of the evening. Do you know which ones they are?"

"Not yet, Mom, but I will learn, and next year I will know every star that you can see. That's what we were talking about." Jackie turned and hugged her mom. "It's so good to have you home. We have been through so much without you these past sixteen years."

"Are you okay, honey? Have you still got that headache? I have not been anywhere, let alone been away for … how long did you say? Sixteen years?" She stood up with a smile and headed inside. At the door she turned and said, "You children—and that means you and your dad—you are always joking around."

Her mom was now back to normal and had forgotten what happened, as Reial had predicted; by the next morning her dad would do the same.

It was now quiet inside, as they had gone to bed, leaving Jackie outside. Looking up at the stars, she saw a comet and made a wish, knowing that it would come true. She heard in the back of her mind, *Are you okay?*

Yes, you?

I'm busy on my next job.

Was that you passing by?

Yes, did you like it?

That was cool.

51

Why don't you come and join me up here?

Can I?

Yes, of course you can.

Oh my gosh, I'll be right up. And with that Jackie disappeared and all that was left was a slight breeze and a feather floating down gently to land on the bench.

Later, as she lay down in her bed she remembered that she had school tomorrow. She took a few breaths in and out, relaxed, and closed her eyes. She could see the sky, and she smiled with tears running down her face. She asked herself, *Do you believe in angels?* and answered, *You bet I do!* She closed her eye, said good night to Reial, and went to sleep.

Good night, Angel.

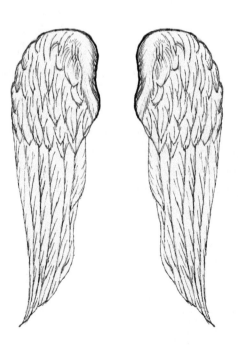

About the Author

K C Copperfield is an inspired fantasy writer developing his ideas from a spiritual perspective. Influenced by other fantasy fiction writers K C Copperfield developed his unique ideas into exhilerating short stories.

CPSIA information can be obtained
at www.ICGtesting.com
Printed in the USA
BVHW07s1730240918
528346BV00001B/145/P